I0529660

A CLOTH HOUSE

a novella by

Joseph Riippi

HOUSEFIRE

www.housefirepublishing.com

ISBN: 978-1-937395-01-8

Copyright © 2012 HOUSEFIRE

Cover art copyright © 2012 Lindsay Allison Ruoff

Interior layout by Lindsay Allison Ruoff

Edited by Kira Clark

All rights reserved. No part of this book may be reproduced or transmitted in any form or by any means, electronic or mechanic, without the written consent of the publisher, except for excerpts for the purpose of review or where permitted by law.

Printed in the United States of America.

The earth is spiraling towards the sun, you know.
Do you understand what these words mean?

For Kyle Barker and Orville Wick

CONTENTS

1983

To Begin

To begin, I grew up on an island. Neither tropical nor desert, neither Virgin nor Bermudan. The trees of my youth were pine not palm. Cones and helicopter seeds might fall, but there was no fear of the coconuts I suspect other islanders endure elsewhere, equatorially.

My Coverings

Mother returned from the kitchen to find her first daughter hidden beneath the folds of a yellow sheet. A flashlight glowing, a muffled titter. What are you doing under there? My young mother asked, frowning and unhappy. I, her invisible daughter, shushed her back. I remember this well. I remember Mother leaving the room.

What I Mean by
I Remember Mother Leaving the Room

What I mean is I remember the sound. Her white
sneakers across the creaking wooden floor slats; her
breathing, sighing, exhalations. She would say she was
in no mood for this. But she never need say such a
thing by that time; I was old enough then to notice the
thoughts behind the words and faces of other persons.
She was Em, 22, my mother, and there was something
about me not right with her. She was 17 when she had
me, 16 when she decided it, 15 at pregnancy's first risk,
not knowing these decisions would mean she would be
mother to this daughter, unendingly. Not knowing she
would never be dancer nor painter nor woman of the
city—none of that which she dreamed. She longed to
be a part of that city on the mainland. But I would be
strange, this daughter. The kind of daughter who never
left the yellow sheet of her own imaginings. Strange
how similar this daughter was to herself, Em might
have thought once. I remember this well. Em did not
remember it.

Husband

He came home announced, riding sounds of gravel and truck. The wind wove through the piney trees. Like sunrise, he would have said. Visitors from the city used words like *clean* or *unspoiled* or *crisp* to describe this wind. Today I remember it the way they described it; the way they described it is the way it still is, reliably.

The Dog, the Daughters' Dog,
Father Had Brought with Him

She would hold her brown head out the truck window and smell the sea salt and pine. She lapped her tongue into and among the strange and saltpiney smells as the truck broke against the drive. Em and her husband and daughters would never have words for these smells the dog tasted. We borrowed the words of others and invent others still for that clean and unspoiled and crispness. But the dog's joy was plain. Father scruffed her ears and neck with hard dirt-covered fingers. She barked from one window and father laughed from the other. Partly as announcement, partly shared acknowledgement of the anticipation and smell of daughter and her yellow sheet, the dog lapping her tongue into the smell of the daughter, and the sunlight that was like sunrise, surfing the wind that was like clean and unspoiled and crisp, like foreign things in the city the visitors spoke of, familiarly.

Em, Almost Elm

Em had not grown used to it, did not need to grow used
to it. She had hardly been to the city, or what one might
call the city if raised from birth on Beach Road North. A
woman cannot grow into that of which they are already a
part, Em might have said. It was as warning that she said
it. She was familiar to this island country in the sense
that familiar is almost family, that Em is almost Elm.
The way a person becomes familiar and unmoved by the
smell of one's own hair, or the pits of self-sweated shirts,
of room temperature. These are things Em never said,
but that I am saying for her now. A person cannot smell
themselves, not like a lover or dog can. This she might
certainly say. And yet still a person's smell is a distinct
thing, distinctly them, theirs, hers. Familiar to family. I
could not distinguish my mother's smell from that of
the yellow sheet. Like pine and soap, like crisp and salt,
it was sewn into and held within that nature. A lovely
smell like loving, of the cloth houses of my childhood,
of what a person leaves and returns to and remembers as
home. And remembers as loving if they are remembering
rightly. Perhaps this was truly how it all was back then.

Lovely and loving, memorably. But perhaps love is only pine and sea salt as I remember them, not as you remember them. Perhaps love is not as it seemed in the house at 1983 Beach Road North, in that same year 1983, before the war that broke us.

Cloth Houses

A girl can live in her cloth house for but a short period. It is to be lived in comfortably in that time and afterwards folded and discarded back to its yellow-sheeted linen closet. It dirties easily. It rips, tears—the real world rushes in and the world of our imaginings must be sutured back with a yellow thread. Another person may find it strange, the sheet stretched above, pillared strong by dining table chairs. A mother can never know the cloth houses of her daughter as well as their owner. But in her own motherly imagining she may construct something almost the same. And Em, she could do this only to an extent, too full of fear to see the light I projected there, the image of her and I swimming against the ferry, backstroking to the city, in parallel, in tandem, cutting through waves, inextricably. Em's cloth house collapsed when she decided to bring me into this world. She became adult, mean and undreaming.

Husband, Home

Em wrapped her arms around him and he wrapped his
arms around Em and she breathed in the smell of his
neck and collar, deeply. She held on longer than usual.
He noticed, but did not say so. She spoke instead: I think
maybe I'm pregnant. She said, I can smell the fish on
you. She said, I can always smell you better when I am
pregnant. She said, Last time, I could smell you so much.
You smelled so hard of fish. He smiled and replied with
squeezing, his father-voice saying she may be pregnant,
but only olfactorily. You can always smell the fish on
me, he said.

1983 Beach Road North

1983 Beach Road North, the address of that first house, the year you spent in our mother's womb. The house one lot closer to the beach was 1985. Still closer, 1987, '89, '91, all in an inevitable rowing to 2013 and the beachfront white-fenced mansion for which our mother would pine. And where I am sitting now as I write this. This was the inevitability Em saw when she moved into 1983 Beach Road North in 1978, the year she was 17 and having me. The years and savings would accumulate, she believed. She would die in a magnificent sunlit room many years past having moved into 2013 Beach Road North. Her husband would pass before her and leave her left to paint away her old age staring at the shells and drifts the falling tide left in its wake. The wind would blow like sunrise across the waves and tidal pools, crisp and clean and unspoiledly. She had a five-year head start when she and my father and me began our lives at 1983 Beach Road North. It was 1978 and 2013 was coming certain as the ebb follows flow, as gravity, as sunrise itself.

Truck

They made love in that truck once, my parents. Just once.
Sometimes they talked about it, tangling their limbs
in bed and cooing. Remember that time in the truck?
One would say this and it would make the other smile
and move his or her hand. It was a favorite memory
of my mother's, she told me on our best day. She told
of driving the island ring road with my teenage father,
listening to guitar music, singing, drinking. It was she
who most often whispered, Remember that time in the
truck? Among those lagging couch pillows watching
television, the dog lapping at their wine glasses, me
curled in my sheets and blankets. It was she who most
liked to remember, then. They believed I did not know
what they were talking about and so they were free with
their words. They did not think I would remember their
sentences like I did. And even if I did, what could I
possibly do with them?

Spill

Something sticky ran beneath the yellow sheet while my
glow and tittering continued. Inside I was an astronaut
or princess riding a spaceship or dragon. Stepping her
white sneakers in the sticky, my mother found this first
daughter had sat on a juicebox or wet her pants or both.
Perhaps she would do better on the next one, she might
have thought, and did not immediately go for the mop.
I imagine she simply touched her belly where you were,
saw in an instant that old widowed woman painting in
the house on the beach.

Truck, Later

I would remember that time in the truck as a teenager,
when I would steal the same truck the night the war
started and Em ran sick to the city. I went after her. We
were living at 1995 Beach Road North then. I remember
remembering my father and that teenage Em as I shifted
the hard gears and tore down the road in tears. There
was grind of dying clutch, the crisp wind flowing cold
outside the window, pine smells, dead dog, road running
for ocean in all directions, waves lapping like a real moat,
death a real dragon, nights falling one after another after
another after another.

Dreamery

Imagining from within walls of yellow sheet. The kind of face my mother was wearing on the other side. The imagining of the something I would do with my life, perhaps a thing greater than what Em had done, a greatness that would get me off of this island. I saw it on the side of that sheet and she saw, on her side maybe, the mirrored opposite of my childhood joy. With everything projected on the sheet that smelled so nicely of pine and soap and my mother, I remember best the sound of her sneakers walking out of the room, leaving me.

The Dog, The Great Lapping Lion Queen

I remember too, well, the sound of the dog's running
paw pads and paw nails against the wood floor like
shells rolling. She lapped up the pee or juice, caring after
neither, enjoyingly. I went on beneath my sheet as she,
The Great Lapping Lion Queen, drank from the moat
of a great princess castle, dragons awaiting the sure,
someday arrival of you, my new sister, with heralds.

Memories, Still

They say it has to do with the way the brain develops, why we can't remember the earliest bits. My first memory is naturally of that yellow sheet, feeling its silky fringe and the way it rubbed bunched and clumped in my palm like wet seaweed. And then pulling it through, that silky part. Feeling the soft coolness between the tips of child's fingers. I still remember the look of it in my fist, wrinkled like a clump of brain. I see it like a kind of still from a film. I remember how much I loved it, relied on it. Father says that in my earliest years on Beach Road North, Em would run that silky part back and forth beneath my nose, ticklingly. He says that when others would come to see the baby, me, she would do this to find my chubby smile. She was so proud of you, he says. Even as small and chubby as you were, you were still so cute, so funny with that blanket. Telling the story to me, so many years after but not so far away, he says it was the surest way to see how beautiful I was, or maybe would be, or maybe might have been, or am still.

1984

Father's Announcement

Father was the kind of man who knew many things. A godly man, too, in his own good way. He announced at dinner that I was soon to have a sister, that you—for whom else would I be writing?—would soon be joining. You are going to have to teach your little sister, our father said. He knew I loved to teach the dog the million island things there were to teach. He knew I already held so much of Beach Road North in my head, and he knew of the cloth houses I hung throughout the trees in our yard, liminally. These were truths and imaginings I could pass on. These were fireflies and fairies whose names I could share. Mountain creeks and rivers we could cross together. Moats and ogres to tame and make friendly. All of this I would tell you, because our father said I should.

The Beginning of the World Is Each Time We Are Born

They stood on the other side of the yellow sheet and wondered what games or wars or adventures I was playing or fighting or loving within that imagination. Father said to Em: As far as that little girl is concerned, the world was created the moment she was born—before that, not a thing exists.

What Em Would Have Said Before Father Continued

Mother would have said something else, something less loving than what our father had said. That is really how I remember her before she got sick, before the war—as less loving but more full of love herself. But before she could have said whatever she may or might not have, our father then would say, did say—for this I remember exactly, definitively, clearly and crisply and unspoiledly—It's like that for each of us, really, Em, like there is nothing before us and nothing after us, and even though we know this isn't really true, it doesn't really matter, does it?

　　　Father was also a man who fancied himself a philosopher.

1977/1985

Sister, you were born in an upstairs bathtub. A midwife
from the city came to 1983 Beach Road North to help at
making sure no one died. I stayed in my room, covered in
a sheet for the full scene. I do not remember my mother
screaming, but I imagine now that there must have been
some of that. That my father must have worried, feared
that I was afraid, seems a certainty. He loved me; he
would not be able to help his worry anymore than he
could help his loving. So he sent the neighbors from
1977 Beach Road North and 1985 Beach Road North
to check on me often. They said things like, Your room!
So lovely! And, What a beautiful fort you've made there
with that sheet—is yellow your favorite color? I imagine
being one of them now, wading into that uncomfortable
silence of the room of a chubby, ugly blonde girl in
a sheet fort, thinking of ways to handle the silence,
frettingly. When I remember the neighbors at '77 and
'85, I cannot help recalling their phony words, how they
tried to distract the reality of what was happening with
whatever I'd made myself. Adults push children further
away from real life sometimes and deeper into dreaming.

And there are so many things I could remember instead, such as their sons and dogs and cars, the pool in the back yard behind 1985 that I once swam in sometime in 1984, when Em's old dreams had fallen one year behind and we were all still living in 1983.

Our Father's God

Our father was a man who believed in the god he saw and heard and felt within his own mind. He kept a postcard from the city's museum in his wallet, a picture of a painting he said was proof of god's existence. This could not have come from a man's hand, he might have said, and by that would have meant that there was a spirit of some kind capable of giving the gift of art or dexterity or luck or love—the love between him and the painting. I, too, was proof of the existence of his god, that much he tells me still today. Our mother, as well, and you, too, he tells of his memories of you often, childishly, gripping his blanket.

Little Darling

I remember he would toss me in the crisp wind and let my blonde hair flop in wavy pigtails among the pines like yellow sunrise, and he would say a loving thing like, You are proof, my little darling, god's little angel. We did not go to church then, and I was never baptized, as you were, nearly. He did not explain much, so I understand his god at that time as a kind of private god, one that did not require a church or congregation but rather just you or me or our mother or a postcard of a beautiful painting— only belief, subjectively.

Grace of Our Father

That night in 1983, when our father announced god
was giving me a sister, we sat around the kitchen table,
said the Catholic grace he and our mother were raised
to say. But it was not of service to a father or son or
holy ghost that we did this, or that our father and we
crossed ourselves before eating or after catching a fish,
or said and did the same after surviving truck crashes or
nightmares. I might have asked him about god then, after
grace, with that girlish innocence of one of god's little
angels, so good at knowing the words of grace by heart,
he would say, but not knowing the reason. He might have
explained god as the thing that decided love, or that was
love. He might have explained that love was the one part
of a person's life they could not in some way control, or
change, or make believe differently.

What Father Says Now About Love

Sometimes these days in the evenings our father and I sit on the porch of 2013 Beach Road North to look out on the body of water that's been the life and death of this family and Father says his philosopher things like this:

You asked me about love, if I could have chosen otherwise, maybe. If I could have left, maybe. But even if I wanted to, I cannot, or could not change that I love you or that I loved your mother, sick as she was, even after what she did. Her war, as you call it. I cannot change that I love the smell of the trees on this island, that I loved that dog of yours. And that I loved hugging your mother in the driveway that evening when she told me she was pregnant again. It's all I have left now, you see, the remembering. I breathe the smell of these trees here and this beach there and remember that night so many years ago just a few houses down. It's still alive, you understand, this love. Knowing that I will die here smelling and remembering this wind makes me happy. Because the love keeps living, you understand? A person can fight everything in this world, my darling. One can kill another out of hate, can hate another, even yourself, so much it kills, as I suspect your mother did. Or a person can do nothing, easily, can simply sit and let the tide carry them off. But you must understand, my darling, my always darling. I could have done nothing with my life, done nothing out of fear of doing something wrong. But I could not help loving the idea of my own family, my own house, my own wife and child, children. That love, that Love that should be capitalized, that LOVE is the god I believe in, that LOVE the only god worth a belief in, I believe. That is the god we said thank you to before we ate each evening. That is the god we thanked after nightmares. That is the god I know will take me away one day, happily, joyously, like a tired crab in a tide pool gets washed away from its shell, fearlessly.

Nothing Like Love or the Ocean

Our mother is dead and there are so many stories she never told. Not full, never finished. Maybe she never meant to. Whether or not she believed she had done sufficient things in life so that it could be considered worth something, for instance, I do not know for sure. I would like to think she believed she had. I work at remembering her that way, if only because a mother deserves to be honored by her children, and because it might change the way others remember her. Life in death is memory only, familiar to imagination, a dead friend not wholly unlike the imaginary friends of childhood we encounter under sheets and in daydream daze. A person can do that, you see. Can work at remembering a certain memory an uncertain way, can mold it into something new, change history, a mother's story. It is not like the love of our father's god, which cannot be helped or changed or forced any more than lapping waves or crisping wind. Memory is nothing like love or ocean.

Em's Second Daughter

Em lay in the tub half-naked and sweaty and exhausted and held her second daughter. This one was beautiful, too, as I had been at first, before my chubbiness became something to be shamed for. But you, sister, were beautiful in a different way, perhaps a better way, with a chubbiness you shed like morning. Em did not want to consider one of her daughters more beautiful than the other, but it was something not to be helped in that moment. I wonder if it took you long to realize this for yourself. Our father loved hard and equally, equanimitably and to the max with all things. But love for Em came on condition of beauty. That she found me beautiful despite my fat is a mark of her motherhood and not something for which she should be praised, even memorably, ever.

Anything Else, Anywhere Else

In truth, I feared very little as a child. Fear is important, you understand. Fear is critical to understanding your past. It is the first thing a child learns from its parents, the trait most often inherited. By writing just now I feared very little, you should take that to mean our mother feared very little, quantitatively at least. One fear only: that insidious dark thought that she would do nothing with her life. Being that I am one of the products of this life, and that she died full of fear, such great fear that I should call it terror, it should go without saying that my own fear now is great and singular. I write this out of fear, fear that if I do not I will be doing nothing from today until I die. Even sitting where she feared she would never sit, I am afraid. And now you, my sister, gone so far away and long ago and still going, I'm afraid you will not understand or see or hear any of this. I am afraid that what I am doing here now will be the same, in the end, as doing anything else, anywhere else.

However, to Put Myself in Em's Situation

If I put myself in the situation of dying, of knowing I would die within a year, a month, a day—as she knew, approximately, assumedly—I do not believe I'd be able to say I had done enough, and I might do something the same as she. A dying person cannot avoid regret, my father might say. But he might save saying that until the very end, to find if it's true or not. He is a man who knows how to save his words.

What Em Would Have Wanted to Do

If she had not been our mother, Mother may have been a famous painter. She painted on stretched canvas sheets, yellow paintings for me and great blue monstrosities of ocean for you. Her belly grew in anticipation of your coming and rubbed sometimes against that paint. She destroyed so many of these sheets, starting over with thick waves of dirty white. Many times she would paint over finished pictures, saying she was ready to start something new. She never considered that she was teaching her daughters that to cover up was the same as starting over, destruction as artful and beautiful a thing as creation.

1996

When I Decided to Leave

I left the island in 1996, the last year our mother was
alive at 1995 Beach Road North. A year behind schedule,
but that remains the house I remember fondest. That
was the year Em became too sick to hide her sickness,
the year I passed 17, the age she had been when she had
me. And then we knew she was sick. She would wake
throwing up. She told my father the smell of fish on him
made her nauseous. She hugged him less and less, until
he drove her finally to the ferry and the city hospital
where they told her she had hidden her sickness too long,
now there was nothing they could do. She hugged him
then and he wept in her ear, for once, atheistically.

What Father Does Now for Fun

Some days, since my return, Father and I sit on the
porch of this beach house and I ask him to tell me
about his childhood. He is almost 70 now, but seems
much older. He tells of his past like it is you and me
he is remembering, not himself. He tells how he loved
baseball and basketball, how he never understood soccer.
He tells of the island parks and their lawns and trees, the
names they went by before our years. They were the same
fields on which we played, but remembered the lives of
different people then. His favorite book, he says, was
that with the boy and the Indian in the woods with the
dog and the river. There are still so many on our shelves
like this. And like his first daughter, his best friend was
a dog named for food. He says his favorite music was
my mother's singing voice, and he means it. I tell him I
don't remember her singing and he says I don't because
she only ever sang for him, and that she did only once
he knows with certainty. I don't say I don't believe him,
but I ask why she only ever sang that once and he says
he doesn't remember. And then we talk about memory.
His favorite thing to do for fun now is to sit on the

porch with me and talk memories. I am fine with this. It's why I moved back, why I bought this house with the money I made in the city. I was done trying to do things for myself and ready for loving my father and this ocean and this road and the memory of this family. This is the thing I do now. We sit on the porch of 2013 Beach Road North and watch the ocean and remember things. He says the more you remember a thing, the more the memory becomes something new and different than the original thing. I always remember Em when he talks like this, and I always want to press for more about her singing voice, but I don't out of kindness. Let him keep the memory pure, I think. But I wonder if we are both remembering her different than she really was, different in an unintended way, and I ask him to verify things. My father says it doesn't matter how it really was, that when he is gone too, I won't know any better, and that's fine by him.

My Favorite Memory of Em

I was a teenager and she was sick and you were gone. She took me by passenger ferry to the city for lunch. She was in a very happy mood and said it was our girls' day out. She didn't seem sick. She was happy to escape the island with me for a brief bit. We saw a movie about ballet dancers overcoming urban upbringings and ate tacos on a city bench overlooking the sea. We looked back at the south shore of our island and she told me things about her mother.

Loving Even the Fall, and Ballerinas

Em said,
        You never met her, but you would have loved her.
She would have loved you, I mean. She would be proud
of you just for being you. A lot of mothers are like that.
Proud of you simply for existing. That's what they meant
in the movie when the mother told the pretty ballerina, I
love you even when you fall.

Talisman

There were boys, of course, on Beach Road North. The
Indian boy at 1985 the one I remember best. He was
my first friend beyond the dog, and he understood the
importance of a cloth hiding place, struggling to make
the world your own, new. Wherever he went he carried
with him a blue blanket, like a cartoon character might,
like a grandfather veteran carries a rabbit's foot, talisman,
a thing disgusting and real and yet believed to have kept
soldiers safe through trenches and wars. Who knows why
we do what we do? Who is to judge?

Swimming

The boy from '85 carried the blanket all places, and in
that year, 1984, we were classmates, shared a bus route,
the only first graders still with our sheets and fears.
We were teased like soldiers never would be, and some
days that summer of '84, his mother took the sheet and
blanket away for laundry, spoke in a not-yelling voice
about how we didn't understand the difficulty of getting
pine sap out of cloth. On these days we would swim
together in the pool behind his house. I remember these
days happily, as one long stream of days. I remember his
child's chest and ribs, his red shorts and gapped teeth
and the pine cones he threw at my head. Later, he died a
grown soldier, blanketless in an Afghan desert, killed by
cold after ejecting from something shot and falling.

Your Sheet, Version

Em gave you a sheet, too, of course. A sheet you could,
like me, stretch over chairs or table legs. You never did
that, this sheet too much smaller, too much more of a
blanket, softer than the yellower version I loved. I don't
believe you would have, even had you lived. Even had
you grown old enough to remember our father tossing
you into the ocean and laughing, your hair blonde and
pigtailed in the breeze, waving.

What I Imagine You Might Have Told About Father

You might have said,
         I remember Father walking me to the beach,
both of us barefoot on the gravel and then grass and then
sand. He lifted me around his neck, gripped me there
hard with a foot dangling from either shoulder before
sprinting at the sea. We hit the waves and it was cold and
I was screaming and smiling too and he was laughing
and shouting my name and yeehaw and Geronimo and
yippee. I can remember tearing back at his hair like a
cowboy at a horse's mane. I remember the water pulled
him down, me with him, sinking and salty. I remember
the gripping of his hands around my calves, hands so
large a thumb could be at my knee and a pinky at the
ankles. I wore a blue hat that knotted beneath my chin,
something Mother made me wear to keep the sun away. I
remember best the shouting, losing my voice, joyfully.

When Em Learned She Was Sick

When Em learned she was sick, she did not tell those of us she lived with. She kept it her secret. She told us other things, like that she wanted soon to be moving. Father was doing well at his job and thought that yes, this was a good idea. And so in 1989 we moved to 1995 Beach Road North, where there would be a pool and five years of happiness, the smell of the beach another six hundred feet strong. But then her secret sick flooded in and drowned us.

What Father Did for Work

Father worked as a salvage diver off North Harbor. There he would sit on his boat with three radios tuned to certain open frequencies, patiently. When a distress call came he would race those others from East and West and South Harbors to the source of it all. The winner won the job. On days of particularly good weather he'd be less likely to hurry, letting South or East Harbors take the work. Enough of the locals knew Father such that he was never desperate of disparate occupations. On days he wasn't working at rebuilding a dock or setting a buoy, he might have sat and smoked and spoke to the fishermen and dockhands and deckhands of North Harbor for hours. He might have retrieved a watch or wedding band that fell between the planks and into the sea. He would do this sort of retrieval for free or for beer. Oftentimes he would offer the paid beer back to the deck or dockhand or fisherman who'd paid it, in celebration at the retrieval of the lost thing. Then, in that final hour of evening before heading home, when they all sat and spoke of their dreams and turned off their radios, they would touch cans and sigh together, contentedly.

How Father Met Em

Father met Em through the swim team at the
high school. She was from a few miles inland, the
neighborhood of rough houses toward West Harbor,
while Father was a Beach Road North man from birth.
Em had always dreamt of living where he did, in a home
where she could paint pottery or pictures or totems from
a top window and look out to a loving husband sailing
into the North Harbor on a strong wind. She loved
Father for the likelihood of this self-imagining coming
true. But in the last years of her war, she loved him
mostly for the memory of the way he kissed at the end
of that first date, the side of her mouth, almost cheekily,
a memory that only got better as it changed with time.
It was almost gentlemanly, almost presumptuous, not
completely either, but memorable as the time in the truck
had once been, too.

What Our Parents Named You

Em never had a name for you. Perhaps she thought she
would look at you and know. But she looked up from the
tub and asked our father if he knew, and then regretted
it. Of course he had an answer. He always had answers.
Em loved that he always had answers. She couldn't help
this love and so it would be he who would name you and
she could not be upset by this. The midwife from the city
smiled and smiled and cleaned and cleaned again and
then did the things our mother supposed her city job had
taught her to do. Our father kissed Em on the forehead,
whispered his own mother's name with a question mark
in its tone. Em nodded. He crossed himself out of habit
or grace for the name he'd given you and said something
like, I already love her or She is so beautiful or An angel
from Heaven, before kissing our mother again and
rushing to tell the news. He found me hiding in my
room, sitting on juice boxes and scaring those women
from '77 and '85.

What I Wish Em Would Have Done

I wish Mother would have loved me the way Father did. Would have loved even the fall and understood me if I'd said I wanted to leave that island and do the things she might have dreamed of doing herself. That is something I wonder about. Besides the skipping of houses down Beach Road North, I know nothing real of her dreams as an adult. I assume at the painting, assume at the pottery. Father, when I ask now, tells me what she wanted most in the world was for happy, healthy daughters. And I try to believe this, but only half-heartedly.

Bad Memories

I don't like to remember this but I must in order to
change it. Must remember it again and again and again:
        You were too young to understand how it had
been on days Father was at his job in the harbor, waiting.
You were too young to know how we weren't allowed
off the street or out the gates that locked Beach Road
North from the highway. How for us the world had to
be made anew each morning because we were trapped
there, Mother's fear never letting us leave by any means
but a cloth house. Only that one time, to the city, to the
movie, which I know now was a way of saying goodbye
to me and the island. You never knew her sick, how for
years whenever we did stray too far we were hit with the
crisp and cold and unspoiled swing of a pine branch—do
you remember? Father doesn't. Father was listening for
other cries and calls for help. And that was the gift our
father's god gave you. The loving memory of nothing.
I'm trying to get you to understand the truth of it, in my
memory at least. And trying to change how I remember,
simultaneously, anticipatorily, prayerfully. Pleadingly
and helplessly. Pointlessly, maybe. I am not sure what I

am doing at all, you see, if you are even able to read this. Perhaps all of the bad was never even real. Maybe all of this is just bad memories changing. Maybe you were never even born.

1984

The First Time We Were Alone in a Room Together

Mother left me in your room and said, Watch the baby.
She did not use your name and I called you by Baby
thereafter. She never liked the name our father gave
you. And there were many things you never liked, too.
That year after you were born you began to almost speak
in whines that were something like language, and you
whined hardest at me. Almost like you wanted to talk to
me. But you couldn't use words yet, would never be able
to, and it made you seem less real to me. It made me feel
mean, too, which was new. I realized I could decide to be
mean, to do mean things. I would say, Mommy, the baby
is whining about something. And Em would say, Stop
whatever it is you're doing, then. And I would stand there
and say, Stop whining, Baby, or else I'll be mean to you.
You would just look back, not understanding, whining.
I never did anything meaner than calling you by Baby.
I threatened, but I am not sure what it is I would have
done.

The Things in Your Room

You died, but there was a yellow blanket that stayed in your crib, even after. You used to grip it like a flag. Your hands were doughy and pink and barely fingered, like the tips of very large thumbs. The wallpaper was covered in shells and seahorses. The rocking horse was a seahorse Father had made. When I tried to ride it in the days after you died, Em shouted at me with the force of all your whines. I kept riding, made a whinnying sound like a real horse. I was riding through the shallow reefs with my dog and fish friends. She had to pull me off. After Father left for work, waving from the truck, Em took me out back and hit me with a tree branch. She said, That's your sister's seahorse, you understand? I didn't understand. I didn't have a sister anymore. I just wanted to ride away more and more after that, be a mermaid.

Other Things in Your Room

Father let me help build a mobile for above your crib. You were still a bump in Em's belly then. I cut butcher paper starfish and assembled them in circles on the kitchen table. Father said things like, Those look great, my angel! And, What pretty starfish! Mother liked you best even then, as just a bump. She said the starfish would scare you. She said to at least make them smile, and when I did, Father said they looked like suns.

The Starfish Mobile

I thought they were pretty, the starfish, even smiling.
Some days on the beach I would sit in full tide pools
with Father and watch the small crabs dance among
the rocks, tip the larger rocks to new spots in the tiny
pools that were like whole worlds but weren't more than
a meter deep. I would wonder what a starfish life might
be like. Some nights Father read to me from books of
how they moved across the ocean floor in constellations,
how they kept the sea clean with what they loved to eat.
I liked the idea of being a fish that was not just beautiful
but clean, too. Em was nicer to me when my room
was clean, would love me more if I were beautiful and
smiling, a sun myself. It would be a better life for me if
I could somehow turn into a starfish that smiled. I must
have known that was a ridiculous wish. But wishes always
come true when we're children. We are told that we can
be whatever we want to be, and we assume our parents
are who they are because they wished it so. Em and our
father were their living wishes come true, and so it stood
they wished for us, too.

How I Made a Cloth House of Your Crib

Father rumbled down the drive with the makings of a
crib in his truck. This would be your bed your whole life.
The boards and slats came together from out a big box.
He carried it up to the room that would be yours while
Mother rested on the couch. She called to me for a glass
of something. I brought her one of orange juice and
she told me not to spill it. I put it on the table next to
her and she said to get a coaster. I went to get a coaster
but she had reached for the glass and I thought she was
holding it when I let go. The glass broke against the floor
like so many fruits. Mother shouted and shouted, but
then stopped and began to cry. I waited for her to say
something but she just kept crying. I went to touch her,
thought that maybe that would help her stop. But she
pulled her arm away and shouted No! Then Father came
down the stairs, saw what had happened. He told me to
go up to your room, to not touch anything and wait for
him. I walked around the broken glass and orange spill
and went. I heard Em sobbing louder as I climbed the
stairs. I heard her shout No! No! No! a few more times.
I remember thinking Father must have tried to touch

her, too. I remember thinking maybe that was the last of the juice. I got to your room and Father had taken the boards for your crib out of the big box. There were clear plastic bags of nuts and screws and plastic black things scattered along the floor. The box was upright, its top open from where he had pulled everything out. It was just short enough that I could climb in and cover the top with my sheet. The light from outside the windows made the top of the sheet glow, comfortingly. I sat in the box for a long time. I tried to think of myself as a starfish, clinging to a rock with the ocean turning over me, the sun shining yellow across the surface of the water. I heard the dog sniffing against the box and I stood and pulled her in. I was a starfish and she was my dogfish protector. We rested and watched the sun pass over, the day pass by, other imagined lights of our own safe world. I miss her, the dog. I wish you had known her better. Em kept her downstairs most of your life, or outside. She was afraid the dog would scare you, would bite you, maybe eat you. But I never believed that. I think Em just didn't like the dog. And so we fell asleep in the box, the dog and me. I don't remember being found, but I imagine it must have been Father who did the finding. Em didn't like to climb the stairs while you were in her belly. She wouldn't have lifted the dog. And I would have remembered if it had been her to peel back the sheet and carry us out of that ocean. She would have been a monster in that imagining.

How Father Let Me Help Him Build the Crib That Killed You

He came upstairs from where Em had been yelling and let me hold things for him. I asked if Mother was okay and he said she was just tired. I remember saying she was always tired now. He said to be nice, she has to watch me all day while he is at work, and we should let her rest now that he is home. He said he would try to be home more from now on and that made me happy. Then we built the crib. He told me what to hold and how to hold it. Hold this plastic piece just like this, my darling. Now let go. Good! Okay, now hold this one, too. Keep it still… perfect! Three more times. I wasn't sure of how this was really helping, but whatever I was doing worked—the crib rose up slowly before us.

Father Could Find Things and Build Things

Father found things for people who lost them. He was
a man who knew how to help other men. And a godly
man, too, like I've said. Like the painter of the painting
he kept in his wallet, he believed he was meant for things
no other man was. If a thing was not lost, then it would
never be found, and therefore, to have it it must be built.
He was a magician, in this way, and could conjure up
cribs from boards and slats, laughter from tears, flowers
from seeds. I wonder if other fathers are this magical to
their children or if I was simply lucky. I have asked him
this, if he believes his god made him a builder above
other men. He laughed in an agreeing way, said no. But
he was nodding, smilingly, humbly.

Some Things I Remember Our Father Building
for 1983 Beach Road North

Father built a family post in the ground to hold our
mailbox. It held the family name, painted with starfish
and seahorse and shells along the letters. The starfish
and seahorse and shells I added, I am told, but I do not
remember doing so. From house to house that post has
traveled with us, numbers climbing toward the beach
where it stands now. Father built the path of ocean
flatstones at 1983, from the driveway to the stairs before
the front door of the house where you lived with us. He
did the same at '95, and some weekend I'll do it here at
'13. He built the porch of which the stairs were a part.
Cedar, red-stained. The porch bench, too, stained the
same. He planted the flowering rhododendrons before
the porch, pink and glowing. He filled the clay flower
pots resting along the porch. He planned the colors
of the flowers in the pots to match the paints on the
shutters bought from a shop in town, to match the 1 and
9 and 8 and 3 wooden numbers at a diagonal beside the
door. The frame for the painting Mother made of the city,
Father built that from four scraps of your crib without
her knowing. The fire in the backyard of your crib, after

it killed you. The rope swing in the oldest elm tree, he lassoed that highest branch with one try. The rope swing in another tree when I wished to swing higher. The fort in the third tree I fell from, and the splint for the arm that broke. A garden patch of railroad ties in a rectangle. Tomato vines, greens and reds. Basil plants. A doghouse. Bowls of his favorite pasta. Pools of olive oil with vinegar, swirling on magic small plates. Fires in the fireplace. Songs from his guitar. Songs from his singing voice. Simple songs I'll never forget. Strong memories. The Pledge of Allegiance. The Star Spangled Banner. Folk songs his father taught him. Church songs his mother taught him. Christmas songs. Christmas presents. Easter baskets. Easter egg hunts. Scrambled eggs on weekend mornings and smiling, star-shaped pancakes in stacks and stacks. Fireworks on the fourth of July. Band-Aids on my cuts or bruises. Chapter after chapter of never-ending happy bedtime stories. Glasses of milk in the middle of the night. Safe cloth houses in the middle of the night. Happy endings to every nightmare. Everything better. Everything brighter, sunnier, definitely. Beautiful flowers for you when you died, and beautiful words after you'd gone. Everything good that ever makes me cry to remember.

Our father was a great builder of things.

1986

How Things Might Have Been Different
if You Had Lived Until 1986

You died in 1985. It wasn't my fault. Or Em's, or Father's.
We were all sleeping. You were almost two years old, old
enough for a bed. You climbed out of the crib Father and
I built for you and somehow you fell. It was a bad crib.
In the morning I found you on the floor with your head
shaped like a piece of fallen fruit, juice bleeding out of it.
I yelled something I don't remember.

How Em Might Have Been Different
if You Had Lived Until 1987

Em's war started the day you died. She began drinking, tithingly. She began cutting. She started hitting. When she hit I thought it was because you were gone and because she loved you best. Or it was because I had helped build the crib that killed you, and Father was too big for her to hit. She blamed us both for letting you die. I can't say I would not have blamed us, too. You had been beautiful and unspoiled, another chance for her. Now I know that in hitting me she had been hitting herself, taking the blame and painting the rest of us with it, which is why I can't believe that badness was ever really real. She was hurting herself most of all, but quietly. I don't know how she hid all the cuts the doctors found on her legs. I asked our father about it when I started writing. He is good at forgetting, a great builder of new memories that let the old stay lost. All he said was:

   I don't remember her doing any of that. She was just sick, my darling. That's all. She died because she got sick, and then sicker, and then there was nothing anyone could do for her. It happens every day, my darling. People get sick and die. I wish she had told us, even if there was nothing we could do but try to love her harder. Perhaps that would have been enough. But I don't know that I could have loved her any harder than I did, and I know she had her reasons. She loved us, is the reason. She didn't want us to worry about her. She wanted us to be happy, safe from pain.

Something Else About Memory

Scientists say a person remembers moments better when they hurt, when there is pain, because of the way the brain works, associatively. You remember not to touch an oven after touching it once. A dog learns not to pee in the house because its owner will scold and drag her outside by the collar. Harsh tones and dragging hurt. Em understood this. It's what made her sick. She hurt me and Father and herself with hitting and cutting, tried to replace the pain of your dying with the pain of other hurts. You understand, don't you? Your dying wasn't your fault, but it hurt her so much. She could never forget. She couldn't think about anything but pain and hurt, this had the opposite effect of healing.

Some Things I Remember Because They Hurt

The first rope swing, the first swing from it. I let go too
late and landed on my back. When I opened my eyes,
sunlight was dripping through the trees like sunrise. I
heard Father come running and then saw his head appear
before the glowing needles. He said, You let go too
late, honey. I pointed at the way the sun came through
the trees and he lay down beside me and agreed, it was
beautiful. Another time I fell from the tree fort. I broke
my arm. Mother had to take me to the hospital in the
city for casting after Father made the splint. Another
time I skinned my knee on the driveway running after
the dog. Another time I burnt my hand making smores
in the fireplace at Christmas. I burnt my other hand
making smores in a fire at a picnic. A fire pit spark once
burnt through my pant leg and into my skin. Bee stings
from the flowers in the pots on the porch. Wasp nests
under the eaves. Bouquets of stings, turning my skin
red as some of the flowers. Rosebush thorns. Blackberry
bushes. Splinters from tree climbing. Falling from tree
climbing. My split lip from running alongside the pool
of 1985 with the Indian boy who would die balletically

in a different fall. Shots in the arm at the doctor's office. Tetanus and measles. Scratching at chickenpox. Scratching mosquito bites. Scratching the scabs that came after. Warts burnt off with nitrogen swabs. Angry pinches under the arm from Em when she was mad and sick. Angrier pinches and slaps when she grew still sicker. A softball to the face. A toe in a doorjamb. Pulling baby teeth. Trimming a toenail too tight. Biting a fingernail to the nub till bloody. Biting the inside of a cheek when experimenting with new ways of chewing. I bit my tongue doing the same. You bit me once, too. Do you remember? For you it was funny and funny is easier to forget. You dying, I remember. Learning Em had died when the sheriff drove up the drive. I am watching Father die now and I am sure I'll remember how it is with him. There are birds crying out in love for each other along the shore, dipping after starfish and dogfish in their tidal pools, oblivious to me. I wonder if I will remember them ten years from now, if I will remember this.

When I Fell in Love

The Indian boy and I sat on the porch of 1985 Beach Road North some year. It was raining, wet sheets falling flatly. The trees bent beneath the rainfall, submittedly, leaving twigs on the blue sheet covering the pool. We watched a seagull walk across the floating sheet and this boy, who would die in desert sand, said, Sometimes I think of the birds in the rain and it makes me wish I was one, that I could fly and swim all at once.

We were maybe twelve years old then, but I think he might have been the closest I came to falling in love.

Hearing the News and the Dread

A sirened truck drove up the drive, announced by gravel
and dread. Father and I hadn't seen Em in three days. The
sheriff had called to let us know he had news and would
be right over. We said, You don't have to come over, just
tell us that you found her and that she will be right back.
He said, It's better if I come in person.

Fireflies

Sometimes the boy from '85 and I would hunt for
fireflies, I tell Father. We are at the beach, the sun is
setting, a firefly lights and unlights before our eyes. Your
mother called them lightning bugs, Father says. You and
I say fireflies, but your mother never did. Really? I ask.
There's no good reason for it, he says. She was from the
island. We say fireflies on the island. Father and I sit for
awhile. A ship moans, a seagull walks by. We watch for
more fireflies. Then I say, We never caught any, the boy
and me. You remember the boy at '85, don't you? Father
nods. No fireflies on the island, he says. I tried to tell him
that, I say.

What I Did After Hearing Em Died

It was 1996 when she finally became too sick to live, and that was the year I left. It took two tries to leave. The sheriff came to say they'd found her body on the city shore. He told us where and it was not far from where Mother and I had sat and talked about ballerinas on our best day. I was 18 and an adult and my mother was dead. That night I made dinner for our Father, his favorite pasta with the basil and tomatoes from the garden. I told him I was sorry. He said, You have nothing to be sorry about. I think I said, I'm going to the city, and I think he said he understood, and that he hoped I would come back. But maybe it was that I just left, took the truck and drove. I don't remember quite right.

What Happened in the Years Between

I got a job and took classes and did what people do.
I dated men and dated women and dated men again,
neither learnedly. I didn't want to love them. I rented
an apartment. I remembered my mother. Some days I
walked to the shore of the city and looked out at the
island. I imagined my mother there swimming, her limbs
cutting through the waves, surviving. I came back on
holidays to visit Father at 1995 Beach Road North. I
bought him a new dog for Christmas one year and we
named him together after a different pasta. We sang the
songs his parents taught and he told about our mother's
singing. I helped him buy a new truck. He tried to get
through a single painting. We went fishing. We walked
along the beach and he told me how we used to sit in the
tidal pools for hours and hours. How I screamed with
joy every time he turned over a rock, revealing the crabs
and snails and fish that had been hiding there. We never
talked of you. It hurt too much and our family had had
enough. Father spent his days at North Harbor with his
radio off, hermitly, never listening for distress calls but
still sometimes diving after lost jewelry. Sometimes he

would drop his own wedding band just so he could go in after it. It was something to pass the time. He tells me that once he found it resting in a seashell like a pearl, and he knew that it was our mother who had done that, it was her saying hello, saying she loved him.

What the Sheriff Might Have Said
About Em's Disappearance and Death

Before I left I asked to see the full police report and hear
the story fully. The sheriff hadn't said how Em had died
when he came to our house. Father wouldn't let him.
The sheriff got the papers and looked them over and said
he didn't want to give them to me. He said, You don't
want to read this, sweetheart. He said, You'd be better off
remembering her how she was. He said, It'd be better if
you just remembered the good times, and honored her
life. Don't focus on how she was when she was sick. He
had good intentions. But if he had had honest ones he
might have said,

        It says here your Father took her to the city
hospital a year ago. He came home and found her in the
bathtub bleeding from razor cuts to the thigh. They kept
her under observation for thirty days, forced her off the
alcohol, gave her medication. It says here that the release
was against doctors' orders. It says your Father insisted
and signed that he would watch her. It says that four
nights ago she was seen at the bar at the ferry landing.
It says the bartender reported she had a few drinks and
didn't say much to anyone. He says she played some

songs on the jukebox before getting on the last ferry across the bay. It says she jumped off somewhere between here and the city. The coroner's report is here too. It says she was found with fresh cuts to the legs and arms and face, that she likely bled out before she drowned, luckily.

To End

Father will die soon. I came back to the island permanently because I know this will happen and I want to remember him better than I remember our mother. I want to remember him in a better way, I mean. And maybe this is a good start, writing this. Often I come to this room where our mother wished to die painting, and I hang a great sheet against the window, like it might have been her canvas. I watch the birds in the rain and think of how someday I will die too, and maybe then I can start over. The new dog might be with me, our father, too. Then the sun will shine through the sheet such that we can see the ocean through its threads, and we can imagine both of you there, swimming in the surf and sheet, dreamily, both so lovely, and we'll remember things that don't hurt quite so much.

᪐

Acknowledgements

Thanks to the Houseburners: Lindsay and
Kira and Rob and Riley for letting me write. Thanks
to Kevin and Matty in Portland for letting me read. To
Sarah in Philly. To John and Edward and Daniel and
Polly and Penina in New York. To Mark in Baltimore.
To Jason and Jesse in Florida. To my family in Puyallup
and my family in Seattle and my family in Texas and my
family in New York and my family in Boston and my
family in other places. And as always to L, the love of my
life.

About the Author

Joseph Riippi was born on a Monday morning in Seattle before the sun rose. He weighed nearly 10 pounds. Somewhere, Kurt Cobain was 16 and maybe writing. On Tuesday, Riippi was incubated. He now lives with his wife in New York City and it's raining.

Joseph is also the author of Treesisters (2012), The Orange Suitcase (2011), and Do Something! Do Something! Do Something! (2009).

HOUSEFIRE

www.ingramcontent.com/pod-product-compliance
Lightning Source LLC
Chambersburg PA
CBHW060944120626
46557CB00003B/1133